The British Are Coming!

by Capers White ◆ illustrated by Tom McNeely

SCHOLASTIC INC.

New York   Toronto   London   Auckland   Sydney
Mexico City   New Delhi   Hong Kong   Buenos Aires

Developed by Kirchoff/Wohlberg, Inc., in cooperation with Scholastic Inc.

Copyright © 2002 by Scholastic Inc.
All rights reserved.   Published by Scholastic Inc.   Printed in the U.S.A.
ISBN 0-439-35161-8
SCHOLASTIC and associated logos and designs are trademarks
and/or registered trademarks of Scholastic Inc.

3 4 5 6 7 8 9 10   23   09 08 07 06 05 04 03

Dear Journal,

I'm Jim Davenport. Together we're going to become famous. You may wonder how an ordinary boy like me is going to become famous. Well, I may be ordinary, but guess what? I'm living in extraordinary times.

It's 1775. King George of England is trying to control the way the colonists (that's us) live. First he taxed practically everything we use. Then he set troops all over Boston.

The patriots (that's another name for colonists) are getting fed up. Why should we pay taxes and obey the king's soldiers? We don't even get a vote in Parliament. Something big is going to happen soon. I can just feel it.

So how's that going to make me famous? With all of this stuff going on, all I have to do is write it down in you, my trusty journal. Then I'm going to put it out there for everyone to read. My title? *The Thrilling Life of James Davenport—Boy Hero.* Now all I need is for something to happen.

April 18, 1775
Dear Journal,

I knew it! Things around here have gotten worse! (Well, better for me.) My big break came last night. Here's the situation. It is 1:30 in the morning. I am lying in the bushes in the town of Lexington—just waiting to record history. "Why the bushes?" you may ask.

It's this way. Last night I woke up to a muffled, faraway noise. I sat up and listened. There it was again. I crawled out of bed and crept down the ladder. I stumbled through the dark to my parents' room.

"Ma, Pa," I whispered. "Someone's comin' towards the house."

"You're dreaming, son, go back to bed," Ma said.

Just then, the noises got louder. Now I could make out the sound of a horse's hooves and a few words.

"Ma!" I cried, jumping into my parents' bed. "It's something about the British!" Then right outside the window, someone shouted, "The British are coming, THE BRITISH ARE COMING!"

By the time the person knocked, my father was up and almost dressed. "Open up! I come with very important news." As Father opened the door, I peeked around the corner. A tall man in boots and a three-cornered hat stood at the door.

"Sir," he said, "my name is Paul Revere. You must prepare to fight. The British are on their way to Concord to destroy our weapons!"

Mr. Revere spoke quickly but clearly. "The British left Boston a few hours ago. Their route will bring them very close to your house."

"What are they going to do?" my mother asked.

"They have two plans. First, they intended to arrest Sam Adams and John Handcock"—two of our most important patriots. "If they capture them, they're going to send them back to England. There they'll try them for treason. Second, as I already told you, they want to seize our weapons. Then we'll have nothing to defend ourselves with."

My father listened closely. "I know what to do," he said. "I will join the other patriots at Lexington Green. We have been preparing ourselves in case the British marched. We can gather there quickly. We are ready to defend ourselves. We need only a minute's notice. We can stop the British before they get to Concord."

My father touched his arm. His voice rang with determination. "Mr. Revere," he said, "I want you to know you can count on me."

"I never doubted that, sir," Mr. Revere replied.

I looked at Pa with pride. He was certainly giving me something to live up to. Tonight was the night to show him that I was a chip off the old block. I decided to go to Lexington Green too. Then I could back him up if he needed help. I'd not only be writing history, I'd be making it.

When Mr. Revere left, my father grabbed his gun. He was ready to go, but my mother jumped up to stop him.

"Oh no," I thought. "If Ma doesn't let Pa go to Lexington, I certainly won't get there." I crept back up the ladder and sat at the top.

Downstairs I heard my mother begging. "Edward, please, you have to think of your family. It is just too dangerous! There are British soldiers everywhere! What if something should happen to you—what would I ever do?"

For a moment my plans faded. Where would Ma be if she lost her husband and her son?

"Sarah, I am thinking of you. This is our home, our land. If we don't fight, we'll lose it. You know I must go."

That decided me. I was definitely going. It would be easy. As far as my parents knew, I was asleep in bed. They would never notice my absence.

I slipped out the window and grabbed a nearby limb of the oak tree. In minutes I was on the ground. I knew the road to Lexington like the back of my hand. I set off.

So, that is what I am doing here. In front of me, a group of patriots are gathered on the Green. And me—lucky me—I'm hiding in a bush close by, waiting for history to start!

I guess I must have dozed off. But let me tell you, if I had known what was in store for me, I would have been too scared to sleep.

I woke up to a sound like thunder. A little frightened, I sat up. Where was I? Oh yes, I remembered. The morning was very foggy. I could barely see. I was cold.

Wait a minute! I gasped. That wasn't thunder, that was marching! Soldiers were coming. I could tell from the sound that there were a lot more of them than us. As they marched closer, I could make out their red coats through the fog. I began to shake.

They wore tall hats that made them look like giants. They marched in one very big, very scary clump. And so many! I thought there were about a thousand but could never count them! Afterwards I learned that they numbered closer to seven hundred. About seventy patriots stood waiting for them on the Green.

What would they do? My heart raced, but I couldn't move. Many of the men were friends of my father. I could even see Pa! I watched and waited. The soldiers kept coming.

Finally I heard a voice. It belonged to the leader of the patriot band—Captain John Parker. "Stand your ground," he said. "Don't fire unless fired upon, but if they mean to have a war, let it begin here."

The British kept on coming. I must have blinked because I don't know exactly what happened next. I just know that someone fired. The war had begun.

All of a sudden, I heard men screaming. I saw them running and scattering. A patriot fell. Then without knowing how or why, I was running too. Bullets whizzed past me. I could hear someone screaming in my ear. Was it me?

I was running with my eyes closed. When I opened them, I got the shock of my life. I was running toward the red-coated soldiers. Their guns were pointed at me. I jolted to a stop.

For a moment I just stood there frozen with fear. Then it dawned on me. I was a little person. The soldiers were aiming high. I dove to the ground. Bullets flew right over my head. I crawled as fast as I could.

Finally, I spotted a barn. A stack of hay stood in the field beside it. I stood up and ran faster than I ever had before. As soon as I was close enough to dive, I jumped into the hay. I burrowed deep into the itchy stuff.

As I lay there trembling, thoughts raced through my head. Why had I ever come? How would I get home? Were the men who had fallen okay? Was my father okay? Would the soldiers be back?

I began to get mad. I thought about my home. The soldiers had walked practically through our farm to get here. I remembered all the work my father and I had done to build our house. Then, all of a sudden, I knew. We were going to win this war! Neither my folks nor my neighbors were going to stand for strangers tearing down our way of life.

As I was thinking, I heard voices. They belonged to Gregory Adams and his friend Eugene, the two bossy boys from my school. I was afraid that if they saw me, they would send me on an errand or something. I kept still and just listened.

"The redcoats got the surprise of their lives," I heard Eugene say. "Our minute men were waiting for them."

"That's right," said Gregory. "It's going to be a long walk home for the British."

I had to get home. I wanted to find out about my Pa. I wanted to protect my Ma and little sister.

15

I finally got home. As I opened the garden gate, my mother ran out of the house. "Where have you been?" she cried, trying to sound angry. Then she ran over and hugged me.

My father had made it home. He wasn't mad either. He knew that I had already learned my lesson. He even wanted my help.

"Get some rest, son. The fight isn't over yet," he said.

Once I was in my room, I put my journal away. One day it will help me tell my story. I don't have time to become famous right now. I have a lot of important work to do first.